For Chloe

Duck
Text copyright © 1988 by David Lloyd
Illustrations copyright © 1988 by Charlotte Voake
Printed in Hong Kong. All rights reserved.
For information address Harper & Row Junior Books,
10 East 53rd Street, New York, N.Y. 10022.

Library of Congress Cataloging-in-Publication Data
Lloyd, David, 1945-
  Duck.

  Summary: A little boy calls all animals "duck"
and all vehicles "truck" until his grandmother
gives him a little help.
  [1. Grandmothers—Fiction. 2. Animals—Fiction.
3. Vehicles—Fiction] I. Voake, Charlotte, ill.
II. Title.
PZ7.L774Du 1988   [E]   87-26200
ISBN 0-397-32274-7
ISBN 0-397-32275-5

  (A Harper Trophy book)
ISBN 0-06-443169-X (pbk.)

Published in hardcover by J. B. Lippincott, New York.
First Harper Trophy edition, 1990.

Duck

Written by David Lloyd
Illustrated by Charlotte Voake

A Harper Trophy Book

Harper & Row, Publishers

There was a time,
long ago,
when Tim called
all animals duck.

"Duck," Tim said.

"Horse," said Granny.

"Duck," Tim said.

"Sheep," said Granny.

"Duck," Tim said.

"Chicken,"
said Granny.

So Granny took
Tim to the pond.
"Duck," she said.

Tim looked and
looked.
"Duck," he said.
Granny kissed him.

A little later
Tim saw a tractor.

"Truck," he said.

A little later
Tim saw a bus.

"Truck," he said.

A little later
Tim saw an old car.

"Truck," he said.

So Granny showed
Tim a truck.
"Truck," she said.

Tim looked and
looked.
"Truck," he said.
Granny kissed him.

For some time after this Tim never said a single word.
He just looked and looked.

He looked at his train. He looked at his truck.
But he never said a single word.

Then Granny took
Tim to the pond
again.
Tim saw the duck.
He looked and
looked.

The duck said, "Quack!"

"Duck," Tim said.
"Duck," Granny said.
Granny kissed Tim.
Tim kissed Granny.